ABOUT THE BANK STREET READY-TO-READ SERIES

Seventy years of educational research and innovative teaching have given the Bank Street College of Education the reputation as America's most trusted name in early childhood education.

Because no two children are exactly alike in their development, we have designed the *Bank Street Ready-to-Read* series in three levels to accommodate the individual stages of reading readiness of children ages four through eight.

- ● *Level 1:* GETTING READY TO READ—read-alouds for children who are taking their first steps toward reading.

- ● *Level 2:* READING TOGETHER—for children who are just beginning to read by themselves but may need a little help.

- ○ *Level 3:* I CAN READ IT MYSELF—for children who can read independently.

Our three levels make it easy to select the books most appropriate for a child's development and enable him or her to grow with the series step by step. The *Bank Street Ready-to-Read* books also overlap and reinforce each other, further encouraging the reading process.

We feel that making reading fun and enjoyable is the single most important thing that you can do to help children become good readers. And we hope you'll be a part of Bank Street's long tradition of learning through sharing.

The Bank Street College of Education

For Doris
—E.S.
For Ellen
—D.O.

To my friends the
Lewises—for all
the hoo-hooing
—L.K.

THE FLOWER OF SHEBA

A Bantam Book/February 1994

Published by Bantam Doubleday Dell Books
for Young Readers, a division of Bantam
Doubleday Dell Publishing Group, Inc.
1540 Broadway, New York, New York 10036.

Series graphic design by Alex Jay/Studio J

Special thanks to James A. Levine, Betsy Gould,
Dilys Evans, and Matt Hickey.

Library of Congress Cataloging-in-Publication Data

Orgel, Doris.
The flower of Sheba / by Doris Orgel and Ellen Schecter ;
illustrated by Laura Kelly.
p. cm.—(Bank Street ready-to-read)
"A Bantam book"—Verso t.p.
Summary: Retells the Old Testament story
in which Sheba visits Solomon
to test his wisdom and recounts
the traditional explanation in which he passes
her final test with the aid of a bee.
ISBN 0-553-09041-0.—ISBN 0-553-37235-1
1. Solomon, King of Israel—Legends. [1. Solomon, King of
Israel. 2. Folklore, Jewish. 3. Bible—Folklore.] I. Schecter,
Ellen. II. Kelly, Laura (Laura C.), ill. III. Title. IV. Series.
PZ8.1.059F1 1994
222'.5309505—dc20
92-33477 CIP AC

Published simultaneously in the United States and Canada

PRINTED IN THE UNITED STATES OF AMERICA

0 9 8 7 6 5 4 3 2 1

Bank Street Ready-to-Read™

The Flower of

Sheba

by Doris Orgel and Ellen Schecter
Illustrated by Laura Kelly

A Byron Preiss Book

A BANTAM BOOK
NEW YORK • TORONTO • LONDON • SYDNEY • AUCKLAND

Long ago, in Bible times,
a great king ruled in Israel.
People said King Solomon was
the wisest man in the world.
He knew the secrets
of the moon and stars.
He knew the secrets in people's hearts.
And he knew how to speak
   with the animals.

Now at this time,
far away in Africa,
lived the mighty Queen of Sheba.
She, too, had great wisdom,
but wanted to grow wiser still.
"Is it true?" she wondered.
"Is King Solomon really
the wisest man
in the world?
I would go to the ends
of the earth
to share his wisdom."

The queen set out on her long journey
at the head of a splendid caravan.
Her servants carried rich gifts
of spices, jewels, and gold.

Drums rolled and
trumpets rang out
as King Solomon bid
a royal welcome
to the Queen of Sheba.
He led her along a path
of gold and silver
to a great feast
in her honor.

That night, they walked in the garden
of Solomon's golden palace.
"Tell me," he asked.
"Why have you come so far?"
"I want to learn from
the wisest man in the world.
Are you that man?" asked Sheba.
"See for yourself," Solomon said.
"Test me."

12

"Then tell me," said the queen.
"What runs day and night
but never gets tired?"
"A river," answered Solomon.
Sheba nodded and asked
another riddle.
"I have a basket of diamonds.
Every evening I scatter them.
And every morning
I gather them up.
What am I?"
"You are the sky,
and the diamonds are your stars,"
Solomon answered.

13

"Have I passed your tests?"
"So far," Sheba said.
"But I have one more."

Her last test took a long time to prepare.
The Queen of Sheba had a hundred artists
make a thousand flowers
out of paper, silk, and glass.

15

She filled the flowers with sweet smells
and planted them in a palace room.
Then, without telling anyone,
the Queen of Sheba hid
one real flower in the room.
"My garden holds a secret,"
she told the king.
"Can you find the one real flower
hidden among all the rest?"

"Of course," said King Solomon.
He looked and looked.
He sniffed and sniffed.
Each flower was lovelier than the last—
but only one was real.
And even the great King Solomon
could not pick it from the rest.
His nose grew weary,
his eyes grew bleary,
and still he had to search.

At last he stopped
and mopped his brow.
"I am warm
from such hard work,"
said Solomon.
He threw open a window
to let a cool breeze blow in.
And he smiled to himself
as a little bee buzzed in.

King Solomon bowed to welcome
the tiny creature.
The queen was puzzled as she watched
Solomon whisper something to the bee.
Then the little bee buzzed
from flower to flower.
It did not rest till it found
a small, pale rose
in a faraway corner of the room.

King Solomon watched carefully.
The little bee settled on the rose
and sipped its nectar.
"Thank you, bee," said Solomon,
and let it sip its fill.

The king plucked the rose
and gave it to the queen.
Sheba thanked him with a bow.
"It is true that God put great wisdom
in your heart," she said.
"For when a mighty king learns
even from a tiny bee,
he is wise indeed."

Drums rolled and trumpets sang out
when the time came for the queen
to return to the land of Sheba.
King Solomon gave her parting gifts
and wrote great poems in her honor.

But the Queen of Sheba
prized one small, pale rose
above all these other riches.
She planted its seeds in her garden.

And forever after,
its sweet smell and golden nectar
spoke of the secret she had learned:
that to the wise,
even small creatures
can be great teachers.